P9-ELW-832

Benjy's Boat Trip

Margaret Bloy Graham

Harper & Row, Publishers   New York, Hagerstown, San Francisco, London

85-100

BENJY'S BOAT TRIP

Library of Congress Cataloging in Publication Data
Graham, Margaret Bloy.
  Benjy's boat trip.

  SUMMARY: A small dog takes a surprise boat trip and meets an angry ship's
cat.
  [1. Dogs—Fiction. 2. Boats and boating—Fiction]   I. Title.
PZ7.G7538Bi   [E]   77-6893
ISBN 0-06-022092-9
ISBN 0-06-022093-7 lib. bdg.

Benjy was a brown dog with long ears

and a short tail. He lived with Father,

Mother, Linda, and Jimmy.

Every summer they all took a trip together.

Sometimes they went to the country,

and sometimes they went to the lake.

Benjy loved trips.

One day Mother said, "We're going
to take a boat trip this summer."
"Is Benjy coming too?" said Jimmy.
"Not this time," said Father. "No pets allowed.
He'll stay with Aunt Mary."
"Poor Benjy," said Linda. "He'll be lonely."

The day of the trip
came. Aunt Mary
and Benjy went
with the family
to the ship. Everybody
on board was happy—
except Benjy and the children.
Then "Visitors Ashore!" came over the loudspeaker,
and Aunt Mary and Benjy had to leave the ship.

All the way
to Aunt Mary's
house,
Benjy
looked out
the car window.

That evening he didn't eat any supper.
He sat right beside the door all night.

In the morning Aunt Mary took Benjy for a walk.

Right away, he slipped out of his collar

and ran straight across town to the waterfront.

A big ship named the *Ocean Queen* was there.

It looked just like the ship his family was on!

Benjy ran up the gangway. No one noticed him—
no one, that is, except Ginger, the ship's cat.
She thought the *Ocean Queen* was *her* ship.

Quick as lightning she tore after Benjy.

He ran behind a big box,

jumped into a hole, and landed below deck.

He hid in a storeroom. Ginger looked

and looked for Benjy, but she couldn't find him.

Down in the storeroom it was dark and quiet.

Benjy was tired. Soon he fell asleep.

In a few hours, the *Ocean Queen*

was ready to sail. It moved slowly

away from the dock. Its whistle blew,

and tugs tooted. But Benjy
didn't hear a thing. He was
still asleep in the storeroom.

After a while, the rolling of the ship

woke Benjy. He went up on deck.

There was water all around. The ship was at sea!

Benjy looked and looked for his family,

but he couldn't find them. It was the wrong ship!

Benjy felt terrible.

He heard the captain say to the mate,

"By golly, there's a dog on board!"

"He'd better look out," said the mate.

"Here comes Ginger. Wait till she sees him."

Benjy didn't wait.
He ran back to
the storeroom
and hid.
He was there
for a long time.
He felt
very lonely—
and hungry, too.
Then he smelled
something
cooking.
It was so good
that he forgot
about Ginger.

He crept out of the storeroom
and followed the smell to the ship's kitchen.

There he found the cook making hamburgers.

"Hi," said the cook. "So you're the dog that came

on board. You look like my little dog at home."

He gave Benjy a hamburger. Benjy was just

going to take a bite when he heard a yowl.

It was Ginger!

He raced out of the kitchen, up some steps,

and into a cabin. It was the captain's.

Benjy ran across the bed. Ginger followed.

"Get out of here!" roared the captain.

Ginger ran out the door, down some steps,

across the deck, and up the mast.

Benjy jumped out the porthole onto the deck.

He ran back to the kitchen,

hungrier than ever.

"Come with me," said the cook,

and he took Benjy to his cabin.

"You'll be safe from Ginger here," he said.

Benjy had a big supper

and went to sleep on the cook's bed.

He slept well all night.

In the morning after breakfast,

Benjy came up on deck. He watched the cook

feed scraps to the screaming gulls.

"Those gulls sound just like cats," said the cook.

"Say, where's Ginger? I haven't seen her today."

He went back to the kitchen,

and Benjy lay down to take a snooze.

He was
almost asleep
when he heard
a cry.
He looked
around.
The gulls
were all gone.

Then he heard
the cry again.
He looked up.
He could see
something
way up
on the mast.

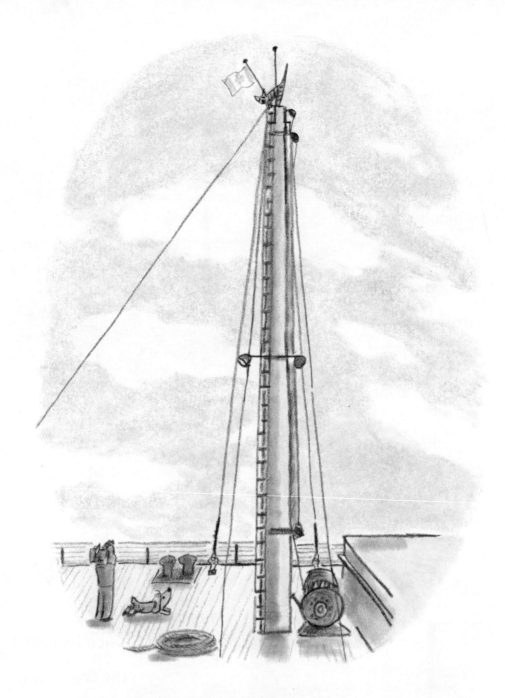

It was Ginger! She'd been at the top of the mast

the whole night, afraid to come down.

Benjy barked and barked. The mate came along.

"What's the matter?" he said.

Benjy looked up at the mast and whined.

The mate looked with his binoculars.

"So that's where Ginger is!" he said.

He took off
his hat
and put down
his binoculars.
He climbed
to the top
of the mast,
got hold
of Ginger,
and put her
inside
his shirt.
Then he
climbed
down again.

"Ginger," he said, "you're very lucky

to have this little dog as a friend."

Poor Ginger just gave a weak *"Meow,"*

and she never chased Benjy again.

From that day on, Ginger was a changed cat.

Benjy enjoyed the rest of the trip.

He spent every morning with the mate on deck,

and every night with the cook in his cabin.

After a couple of weeks, the *Ocean Queen*

returned to Benjy's hometown.

As the ship came into the harbor,

Benjy could see all the places he knew.

He ran back and forth on the deck and barked.

He'd had a wonderful time on the ship,

but now he was ready to go home.

The minute the gangway was down,

he ran off the ship and along the dock.

The cook and Ginger saw him go.

"Good-bye, doggie!" shouted the cook.

Benjy stopped, looked around, and barked.

Then he ran straight home.

The family was very, very happy to see Benjy.

"Aunt Mary thought you were lost,"

said Linda. "She cried and cried."

"But *we* knew you'd come back," said Jimmy.

"Look," said Linda. "We brought you a present."

It was a toy ship that went
round and round in the bathtub.

Benjy loved it. It reminded him
of the *Ocean Queen*.

On a walk a few weeks later, the children
and Benjy heard a ship's whistle. Benjy pulled
the children all the way to the waterfront.
There was the *Ocean Queen* leaving the dock,

and the cook and Ginger were on deck!

Benjy jumped up and down and barked.

"Benjy sure likes ships," said Jimmy.

"On our next boat trip he's coming too,"

said Linda. "We won't leave him behind again!"

And they didn't.

The End